BAND GEEKS

Settling the Score

Calico

An Imprint of Magic Wagon
abdopublishing.com

by Amy Cobb
Illustrated by Anna Cattish

For Sheba.
And with sincerest gratitude to Mr. Vaught, who has instilled a love of music in the hearts of many. —AC

abdopublishing.com

Published by Magic Wagon, a division of ABDO,
PO Box 398166, Minneapolis, Minnesota 55439.
Copyright © 2017 by Abdo Consulting Group, Inc.
International copyrights reserved in all countries. No part of this
book may be reproduced in any form without written permission from
the publisher. Calico™ is a trademark and logo of Magic Wagon.

Printed in the United States of America, North Mankato, Minnesota.
102016
012017

Written by Amy Cobb
Illustrated by Anna Cattish
Edited by Tamara L. Britton & Megan M. Gunderson
Designed by Christina Doffing
Art Directed by Candice Keimig

Publisher's Cataloging-in-Publication Data

Names: Cobb, Amy, author. | Cattish, Anna, illustrator.
Title: Settling the score / by Amy Cobb ; illustrated by Anna Cattish.
Description: Minneapolis, MN : Magic Wagon, 2017. | Series: Band geeks
Summary: The Benton Bluff Junior High band's loyalties are divided
    between director Mr. Byrd and a new student teacher.
Identifiers: LCCN 2016947368 | ISBN 9781624021756 (lib. bdg.) |
    ISBN 9781624022357 (ebook) | ISBN 9781624022654 (Read-to-me
    ebook)
Subjects: LCSH: Bands (Music)--Juvenile fiction. | Junior high schools--
    Juvenile fiction. | Middle schools--Juvenile fiction.
    Classification: DDC [Fic]--dc23
    LC record available at http://lccn.loc.gov/2016947368

TABLE OF CONTENTS

20.00

3-9-18

Mid America

Chapter 1 MUSICAL SCORE p. 4

Chapter 2 CALL ME NATALIE p. 15

Chapter 3 BAND BINGO! p. 25

Chapter 4 UNIQUE GEEKS p. 35

Chapter 5 A BAND DIVIDED p. 47

Chapter 6 STOP & LISTEN p. 58

Chapter 7 HOLIDAY PLANS p. 69

Chapter 8 TAKING CREDIT p. 80

Chapter 9 IN THE SILENCE p. 91

Chapter 10 THE BIG DEBUT p. 102

Chapter 1
MUSICAL SCORE

"I have an exciting announcement to make!" Mr. Byrd, our band director, clapped his hands to get our attention. "As many of you are aware, there's only one month until winter break."

That's all it took to get the whole room buzzing. Everyone started talking all at once.

"Hey, Carmen! You can always tell it's almost winter break when Byrd breaks out the holiday beach shirts," Davis Beadle said to me.

This was my first year in room 217, the Benton Bluff Junior High band room. And that was one of the first things I'd learned. Mr. Byrd always showed up to class in tropical shirts, khaki shorts, and a straw hat. The colder temperatures didn't stop him either. Today, seashells were arranged on a sandy background, but *Ho! Ho! Ho!* appeared, festively, as well.

"Before buying that shirt, Byrd should've said 'No! No! No!'" Davis ended his joke by tapping his drumsticks on his snare drum.

"That was bad, Davis. Really bad," I said, holding my own drumsticks to form a giant *X*.

"Maybe, but you smiled."

I shook my head, trying not to encourage him. Davis and I were both in the percussion section. I'd gotten used to his corny jokes. Plus, I knew he didn't really mean anything by it. Davis loved Mr. Byrd, just like everyone else in band did.

"Quiet down!" Mr. Byrd said then, giving a shrill whistle to get everyone's attention. Silence fell across the room, and he went on, "As I was saying, I have exciting news. A local theater is preparing a production called *What's Your Holiday?* to showcase the diverse ways people celebrate the season. Our band has been asked to participate."

"I knew it!" Miles Darr said. "We're going to be famous!" Miles was our band's self-appointed public relations guy. He made and uploaded online videos of our performances all the time, hoping we'd get discovered. So far, it hadn't happened. And honestly, half of the viewer hits were from Miles and his mom watching his videos over and over again.

"Slow down, Miles," Mr. Byrd said. "This is a small community production that probably won't bring Hollywood agents knocking on our band room door."

Miles looked disappointed.

"But it will be a great opportunity for us," Mr. Byrd added. "Since we only have a month until our big debut, I have appointed a theater committee to work on some ideas. When I call your name, please come forward."

Mr. Byrd reached for a clipboard on his desk and read, "Miles Darr."

"Yes!" Miles said, pushing his wheelchair to the front of the room.

Mr. Byrd smiled and went on, "Hope James, Sherman Frye, Colby Ellis, come on down!" The way he said it reminded me of my nana's favorite game show, *The Price is Right.*

They all followed Miles and lined up beside Mr. Byrd.

"And our fifth committee member is Carmen Trochez," Mr. Byrd finished.

"Me?" I asked, pointing at myself to make sure I'd heard it right.

"Yes, you!" Davis said. "Boy, your face is as pink as the flower in your hair."

Davis wasn't joking about that. My face felt all steamy as I made my way to the front of the room to join the others. It didn't help when Zac Wiles stood up and started a round of applause.

See, being the center of attention wasn't my thing. At all. That was one of the reasons I liked

playing drums. People heard us, but they weren't staring at us. I mean, who practiced in the very back of the band room each day? And who stood in the back row at concerts? The percussion section, that's who. That was just the way I liked it.

Mr. Byrd held up his hands, and the applause died down. "Section leaders, please warm up your groups while I go over a few things with the committee," he said. Then he turned to us. "You may be wondering why I selected you all."

"I am," I said. "I don't know the first thing about the theater."

So Mr. Byrd said that Miles had pizzazz. Hope brought order to the band. Sherman's energy was catching. Colby was creative. And that left me.

"Carmen, you're our glue," Mr. Byrd said.

"That means you're sticky," Sherman said.

"Sort of. It means Carmen holds things together," Mr. Byrd explained. "She not only keeps a steady beat with her drum, but she's steady in her interactions with the rest of the band. Sometimes people like that are called peacemakers." He smiled. "Every committee needs a peacemaker."

That made me blush all over again. I was relieved when Hope raised her hand, moving the attention off of me.

"Yes, Hope?" Mr. Byrd said.

"What exactly will we be doing?"

Mr. Byrd pulled out a pamphlet. Big, bold letters across the front asked the question, "What's Your Holiday?" Beneath that were pictures of different kids. Some celebrated Hanukkah. Others celebrated Christmas, Ramadan, or Kwanzaa.

"What's this holiday?" Sherman asked, pointing to one of the photos.

I knew. "That one is called Ramadan. It's a holy month for Muslims."

"You're right, Carmen," Mr. Byrd said. "It's based on the lunar calendar, so it falls on different dates each year."

"Miss Delgado said in science class that *lunar* means 'moon,'" Hope said.

Mr. Byrd nodded. "Ramadan ends with a three-day festival called Eid al-Fitr, where Muslims have special prayers and meals. Sometimes they exchange gifts, too."

"Cool!" Sherman said.

It was cool. But I wasn't sure yet if this theatrical production would be. "I've never acted in a play before," I said then.

"That's fine because you won't actually be acting," Mr. Byrd said. "The theater has already held auditions, and both kids and adults from across the community have been selected for those roles. But the director, Mrs. Dillingham, hoped adding music to the production would add to the holiday vibe. That's where you come in. Check this out."

Mr. Byrd handed each of us the production's script. Sections were highlighted, and notes were written in the margins. Stuff like, "Insert song here."

"This is sort of confusing," Hope said.

"Basically, Mrs. Dillingham is allowing us to select some songs we'd like to play. We'll also combine instruments to create a combination of sounds to add to the various scenes. And in some instances, we've been asked to find everyday objects to create various sounds."

"It sounds like a lot of work," Sherman said.

Mr. Byrd nodded. "It is. But with an entire month to plan, I believe we have time to create a musical performance we can all be proud of.

"A logical starting point would be for you all to look over the script and then select some music you feel best fits with the scenes. From there, you can begin playing around with the different instruments to see which ones work well to add a musical element to these highlighted scenes."

"I think I get it," I said. "It's like in a horror movie when there's creepy music playing to scare people even more. Or upbeat songs play in happy scenes."

"Exactly!" Mr. Byrd said. "In movies, the musical selection is referred to as the score."

Colby launched into playing air guitar and sung a few lines he made up on the spot. "Benton Bluff Junior High is writing a score. We've gotta make it good. It can't be a bore!"

See, to Colby, life was one giant musical. And he was the star of his own show. He turned any phrase into a tune. Colby played saxophone in band, but he excelled at all of the air instruments— guitar, flute, trumpet. You name it.

"Creating our own score sounds pretty fun," I said. And I wasn't just saying that. Now that Mr. Byrd had explained it, I was excited about working with the band for the theater production.

"I think it'll be fun, too." Hope smiled.

Someone knocked on the band room door then.

"Class, I almost forgot I have another surprise to share with you," Mr. Byrd said.

"Another one?" Sherman said. "I hope it's good."

"Me too," I agreed. Mr. Byrd was full of surprises. Some were good, like the time we took a field trip to a recording studio. And some were not so good, like pop quizzes matching band vocabulary words to their definitions. I wondered which kind of surprise this would be.

Chapter 2
CALL ME NATALIE

"Today, we have a special visitor in room 217," Mr. Byrd went on.

"Is it Rube?" Kori Neal asked. Everyone knew the locally famous jazz musician Rube Chenault. He had a store called Jazz Front in town where a lot of band kids went to hang out. And Kori was always talking about how Rube helped her shine up Russell, her school-loaner trombone.

Mr. Byrd shook his head. "That's a great guess, Kori, but it's not Rube this time."

"Aw, man!" Kori looked disappointed.

"I think you'll all like this guest, too." Mr. Byrd opened the door.

In sashayed a girl who was *fashionable*! I loved her designer jeans. The green purse slung over one shoulder perfectly matched her hoop earrings. And the Peter Pan collar on her shirt was super cute.

"Who is she?" I said to Hope, Miles, Colby, and Sherman. We were still up near the front of the room.

"Maybe she's a new student." Sherman smiled all weird. "She's kind of cute."

Miles and Colby must've thought so, too. They had goofy grins on their faces, just like Sherman.

"Snap out of it," Hope told them.

"Yeah, there's no way she's in junior high," I said. "She looks a little older than my sister, Rayna. And Rayna's a high school senior."

"Everyone, I'd like you to meet Natalie Tate," Mr. Byrd said then. "Miss Tate is a student teacher, and she will be spending the next few weeks with us in our band room."

Sherman's smile got even bigger. "See? She is a student," he said.

"Not just a student, but a student teacher. That means she's in college," I said.

"Too bad. I think I was in love." Sherman made a heart with his pointer fingers and thumbs.

Hope pretended to karate chop Sherman's heart. "Now it's a broken heart. Get over it."

"Someone's jealous." Sherman pointed at Hope.

Hope rolled her eyes. She and Sherman didn't always get along so great. That's because they both played the flute, and they both wanted to be the best to earn first chair.

Miles looked at me, like I was supposed to do something to make Hope and Sherman stop. At first, I wasn't sure what to do. But I got an idea. I stepped between them, so they couldn't see each other. That always worked with my cats, Stoffie and Mesa. And it actually worked with Sherman and Hope, too, because they quit arguing.

Miss Tate waved at everyone. "You can call me Natalie," she said.

"Wow!" I said. "I've never had a teacher who let us call them by their first name before."

"Me neither," Miles said. "But extra, super famous musicians only use one name, you know."

"Like Madonna," I said.

And Hope added, "Or Beyoncé."

Colby started air drumming, like he was going to start singing one of their songs. But then Mr. Byrd asked everyone to go around the room and introduce themselves to Natalie. Lilly Reyes started off the introductions in the woodwind section. After that, the brass section introduced themselves, and Davis ended the introductions in the percussion section.

"Don't forget us, Mr. Byrd!" Sherman waved his hand and bounced up and down to make sure Byrd noticed him.

"I could never forget you, Sherman." Mr. Byrd smiled. "Natalie, this is our newly formed theater committee. Meet Sherman, Carmen, Hope, Miles, and Colby."

We each waved as Mr. Byrd said our names.

"This group is working on creating a sort of musical score for an upcoming theater production called *What's Your Holiday?*" Mr. Byrd said. Then he told her all about our project.

Natalie shot us a thumbs-up and said, "That sounds awesome!"

"Hopefully our performance will sound awesome, too," I said. Since Mr. Byrd had selected me to be a part of the committee, I didn't want to let him down. Or the rest of the band either. Or everyone who came to the production. Then it hit me—there would be a ton of people there.

"I'm sure Mr. Byrd wouldn't have suggested you participate if you couldn't handle it, right?" Natalie said, smiling. "You'll do great!"

I smiled, too. "Thanks!"

"Natalie, we're just about to begin practice. Today, you'll just be observing our class. Correct?" Mr. Byrd asked.

"Observing!" Sherman cut in. "So you're going to be spying on us?" He wiggled his eyebrows up and down.

Natalie laughed. "I won't exactly spy on you, Sherman. I'll take notes on the setup of your band room, Mr. Byrd's teaching style, and how he interacts with you students."

"Interesting. But what's with the luggage?" Sherman asked. "Is that your spy gear?"

I nudged him. It was sort of a rude question. But by now, we were probably all wondering why Natalie had walked in pulling a case on wheels. It looked sort of like the luggage I'd taken to band camp last summer.

"This," Natalie said, "is my homework." She popped open her case so we could see the stack of papers crammed inside. "No spy gear. See?"

Sherman leaned in for a closer look. "Aha! I see *Student Worksheet* typed at the top of that paper right there." He pointed. "You are spying on us."

Once Sherman got an idea stuck in his head, there was no stopping him. "I'll tell you all you need to know about me. I'm thirteen. And I'm practically an Olympic yo-yo-er." He pulled out a green yo-yo and did some tricks to prove it.

"Cool!" Natalie said, obviously impressed by Sherman's walking the dog trick.

But Mr. Byrd didn't look quite as impressed. "Okay, Sherman. That's enough," he said.

Sherman always had tons of energy. Like, he even did warm-ups before band practice each day. I'm not talking about warming up his flute by playing up and down different scales, either. I mean real warm-ups, like jumping jacks, toe touches, and squats.

At the beginning of the year, he even got a lot of us new band kids to warm up with him. Even me. That lasted until I noticed that none of the older band members joined in. Talk about embarrassing!

Anyway, Sherman never knew when to stop. Like now. So before he got into trouble with Mr. Byrd, I said, "Come on, Sherman. You can show off some more of your tricks later."

"That's right." Mr. Byrd nodded. "I'm afraid if we don't get practice started soon, you're going to have a lot of extra practice at home tonight. So if you'll please join the rest of the band, we'll begin."

Sherman shoved his yo-yo back into his pocket. And while Colby, Hope, Sherman, Miles, and I went back to our sections, Mr. Byrd helped Natalie get settled to begin her observations.

"I can't believe it," Davis said when I stood behind my snare drum, next to his. "Now we have two teachers in one class." He looked upset. "I'm no math whiz, but even I can tell that doesn't add up in our favor."

"It'll be cool," I said.

"Are you kidding?" Davis said, nearly dropping his drumsticks. "It's so not cool! We'll have double the practice, double the rules, double the everything."

I hadn't thought about it like that. But still, Davis was probably upset for nothing. "Natalie's not a real teacher yet. She's just here to learn how to be a real teacher," I said.

"You've never had a student teacher before, have you?"

I shook my head.

"Well, I have. In fourth grade," Davis said. "Mr. Minotti breezed in one day, and fourth grade was never the same again. I almost quit school."

"Davis!" I said.

"I'm not kidding. He had me so mixed up about the multiplication tables! That summer I had to get a tutor to catch back up."

I glanced toward the front of the room, where Natalie was talking to Tally Nguyen, Yulia Glatt, and some others. She was all smiles with them.

"But she seems nice," I said.

Davis frowned. "Mr. Minotti did, too. For, like, the first day."

"I'm sure there's nothing to worry about," I said. "We probably won't even know she's here."

Davis shot me a funny look. I could tell he didn't believe me.

Chapter 3
BAND BINGO!

But I was right. For the rest of the week, we hardly noticed that Natalie was in room 217. She mostly sat at Mr. Byrd's desk, observing us and taking a bunch of notes every day. The next Monday, though, that all changed.

"Students," Mr. Byrd began when everyone was assembled in the band room, "I'm sure we've all enjoyed having Natalie with us."

Some people clapped, and a few even cheered.

Mr. Byrd smiled. "She still has a few more weeks here," he went on, "but beginning today, she'll play a bigger role in our classroom. Natalie has planned some lessons for you, and she'll lead band class just like a regular teacher. I know you'll all give her your full attention."

Mr. Byrd looked at Natalie then. "They're all yours."

Davis elbowed me. "What'd I tell you? It's like that thing with Mr. Minotti all over again."

"Just give her a chance," I said. Besides, Davis was probably exaggerating. Natalie couldn't be that bad.

"Thank you, Mr. Byrd," Natalie said. The heels of her super cute boots clicked across the floor as she headed to the front of the room. "I have a lot of fun lessons planned for you guys."

I expected Natalie to direct us from the podium at the front of the room, just like Mr. Byrd always did. She didn't. Instead, Natalie reached into the rolling case she always wheeled around with her and pulled out a box. "Who wants to play Band Bingo?" she asked.

"Me!" Several hands shot up across the room.

"Bingo? Really?" Davis said. "She's gotta be kidding. What are we anyway, kindergartners?"

"No, but you do act like a kindergartner sometimes," I teased. "Just the other day you pretended to pick your nose with your drumsticks."

Davis crossed his arms. "Ha, ha. Not funny," he said. Then he smiled because he knew it was true.

We didn't even take out our instruments. Natalie had us move chairs around and set aside our stands. Then she handed out bingo cards.

Instead of numbers, like regular cards, the Band Bingo cards had pictures of different musical symbols and terms, like *chord*. Mr. Byrd had taught us that a chord was three or more notes played at the same time.

When everyone had a card, Natalie said, "Okay, let's begin. Put your marker on the Free Space in the middle. If your card has what I call out on it, then you'll mark it. Like this." She demonstrated.

"Oh, brother. What's next, Band Simon Says?" Davis asked. "Simon says, 'Give me a beat.'"

"Hey, that could be fun," I said.

Davis shook his head.

"Let's play," Natalie said. "And remember, the winner is whoever gets five spaces covered in a row. Here we go!" She held up a picture. "Who has a whole note?"

"Not me," Davis said.

I eyed my card. "I do!"

After a few seconds, Natalie held up a picture of five black lines. "Next is a staff."

"I've got it," Davis said, marking his card.

I didn't have that one.

"Now we have the word *maestro*," Natalie said.

"I know what that means," Sherman said. "That's a great conductor or music teacher."

"Like Mr. Byrd! He's a maestro," Hope said.

Mr. Byrd smiled. "Why, thank you, Hope. But please pay attention." He pointed toward Natalie.

She went on with, "Who has a quarter rest?"

"I do," I said. It kind of looked like a zigzagging lightning bolt.

Natalie held up another picture. "Everybody probably recognizes the treble clef, right?"

I had that one, too. It looked like a fancy *G* with a line going through it that had a teeny round ball on the bottom. Now I only had to mark two more squares and I'd have five covered in a row to win.

Too bad I didn't have *tune* or *adagio*, the words Natalie called out next. But when Natalie held up a picture that looked like half of a heart with two dots behind it, the bass clef, I had that one. After that, she held up a half note. I had that on my card, as well.

"Bingo!" I said.

At the exact same time, Sherman and Tally yelled out "Bingo!" too.

"I said it first," Sherman said. "So I'm the winner. Right, Natalie?"

"You're all winners! Let's give them a hand," Natalie said.

Sherman stood up and bowed. "Thank you, thank you."

"You won too, Carmen! Take a bow," Davis said.

I shook my head. "No way!" Just thinking about it turned my face red. I didn't have the guts to do stuff like that. I wished I did. Sometimes I pictured myself saying funny things like Sherman or acting cool like Hope. But it never actually happened.

We played a few more games of Band Bingo. Davis won a game. Hope and Colby did, too. Then right before class ended, Natalie reached into her case again. This time, she pulled out a handful of worksheets stapled together to make a booklet.

"Please pass these around until everyone gets a copy," Natalie said.

Lemuel Soriano's hand shot up.

"Yes, Lem?" Natalie asked.

"I think you made a mistake," he said. "The first worksheet has a picture of a clarinet, and I play trumpet."

Natalie shook her head. "There's no mistake," she said. "I know you play trumpet. But I think it's important to learn about other instruments, too, even if it's not the instrument you play. Does that make sense?"

Lem didn't sound so sure when he said, "*Oui, mademoiselle.*" His family was from the Philippines. And Lem told me that his family tree included some French royal ancestor about a bazillion years ago. That's why he used French words every chance he got. Only so far, Lem didn't seem to know that many words.

Natalie continued, "These worksheets have diagrams of different band instruments. Your assignment is to write the correct name for the parts of each instrument. For example, here," she pointed to the clarinet worksheet, "you would write *bell*. Be sure you color the instruments, too."

"Coloring sheets?" Davis looked like he couldn't believe it. "She really does think we're five."

"Don't worry about it, Davis," Colby said. "At least she didn't assign tons of practice pages for homework, like Mr. Byrd does."

Hope must've overheard. "It is band, you know," she said. "I'd rather practice our sheet music than color saxophones and French horns any day."

I skimmed through my booklet. "It doesn't look that bad."

"And I have one more worksheet for you," Natalie said then, holding up another stack of papers. "This one is a little different, though. I'd like to get to know all of you better. Please read each question and tell me more about yourselves." She passed those around, too. "Plan to turn everything in by Friday."

"I thought she said her lessons would be fun," Davis said. "Worksheets are totally un-fun."

"And a real time waster," Hope added. "Some of us actually like practicing our instruments at home. I mean, hello! That's why we joined band."

"You got it!" Davis fist-bumped Hope.

Davis and Hope seemed like they were being sort of hard on Natalie. So I said, "This is only her first lesson. The next one will probably be better."

"I doubt it," Davis said. "You also said we probably wouldn't even notice Natalie was in the classroom. Remember?"

I shrugged. "I remember. But you should also remember that Natalie's a student. She's still learning, like us."

"Exactly!" Colby said.

"Hey, guys!" Kori came over just as the bell rang. "A bunch of us are heading to Jazz Front after school to tackle all of our worksheets together. Do you want to come?"

"Sure," I said. "That sounds good!"

Davis and Colby both said they'd be there.

"I'll come, too," Hope said. "But forget tackling worksheets. We should figure out a way to get Natalie out of our band room. ASAP."

"Yeah," Davis agreed. "She needs to pack up her bingo box and head to the preschool class."

Hope laughed like Davis had made the most hilarious joke ever. Colby didn't seem to think it was funny at all. And Kori looked like she didn't know whether to laugh or not.

What was going on in room 217? It was like people were taking different sides. That wasn't good. A band that didn't get along was like a bunch of out-of-tune instruments. The harmony stunk.

Chapter 4
UNIQUE GEEKS

The bell above the Jazz Front door jingled when I went inside that afternoon.

"Howdy do!" Rube said from behind the glass counter filled with vintage jazz photos and albums.

"Hey, Rube! How's it going?" I asked.

"Better now that all of you kids stopped by to liven things up. When y'all aren't around, I tell you, it can be mighty boring." He smiled before turning to ring up a sale.

"Carmen! Over here!" Miles waved me over to our usual table beneath a window.

When we could get our parents to drop us off, Jazz Front was our after-school hangout. If Rube wasn't busy waiting on customers, sometimes he hung out with us, too.

The store was super cool. Posters of old jazz musicians, like Louis Armstrong and Duke Ellington, dotted the walls. Vintage instruments on display gave the place a funky vibe. And jazz music played softly from the speakers overhead.

"Hey, guys!" I said, sliding out a chair between Hope's seat and Miles's wheelchair.

"Hi, Carmen," Colby said, sliding over to make room. Sherman and Kori were already gathered around the table, too. They'd all started on the booklets Natalie handed out in class.

I pulled a pencil from my backpack and got busy filling in the diagram on my saxophone worksheet. I didn't know all of the parts, but I knew who did. "Colby, what do you call the shiny gold thingy that holds your reed in place?"

"That's a ligature," he said.

"Thanks!" I said.

He smiled. Then he sang some song he made up on the spot about helping friends.

"Shhh," Hope shushed him. "I can't concentrate. And I'm stuck on the trumpet. With all of its valves and tubes, it's like some kind of weird maze."

Miles glanced up from his worksheet. "It is sort of confusing. I'll help you." He pointed out the different valves and valve tuning slides.

"Hang on a sec!" Kori said, flipping to the trumpet sheet in her booklet. "I'm going to jot that down, too."

"Me too!" Sherman said.

Then I got an idea. "What if each of us tells the group the parts of our own instrument? We can get the diagramming done in no time."

"I like it!" Davis said.

So we took turns explaining the parts of our different instruments. Since Miles was already telling us all about his trumpet, he went first. Then Kori told us about the trombone. Colby filled us in on the saxophone. And Sherman and Hope worked together to tell us about the flute.

"That leaves our snare drum, Davis," I said. So we agreed that I would tell everyone about the parts of the drum itself, and Davis would tell them about the drumsticks.

"I didn't even know a drumstick had different parts," Sherman said.

"Sure it does," Davis said. He pulled a drumstick from his backpack. "See," he said as he pointed, "the tip is small compared to the shoulder."

"I see it," Colby said, filling in the drumstick diagram in his booklet. "You know, I've never paid attention to that before."

"People might think they're just sticks," Davis said. "But there's more to them than that. When a drummer plays, the sticks have to be balanced. It might even help you hit the sweet spot on a drum."

"Sweet!" Sherman said.

Everyone laughed. And Davis looked sort of proud that he was able to teach the others about the instrument he loved.

This was nice. Super nice. I was worried back in the band room earlier when Kori first said we were meeting at Jazz Front after school today that this wouldn't go so great. But now that we were here, everyone was working together. And so far, nobody had said anything about Natalie at all. Maybe everyone just needed time to cool off.

"Now we only have one sheet left," I said, reaching into my backpack again. "The worksheet about ourselves."

"This'll be easy," Sherman said.

I thought it would be, too. I mean, who knew us better than ourselves. Right? But it turned out some of the questions were sort of tough.

Some of the others must've thought so, too. Because after a few minutes, Sherman asked, "What makes me unique?" He tapped his pencil eraser on the table while he thought about it. "I know!" He rolled up his shirt sleeves and flexed his muscles. "It's these."

"Seriously? Your flute has bigger muscles than you," Davis joked.

Sherman acted all offended, but he joined in when everybody laughed. The truth was, Sherman was the skinniest kid in the band. He was sort of built like his flute, now that Davis mentioned it.

When everybody stopped laughing, I said, "I know what makes you unique, Sherman. You're the only person I know who can yo-yo."

"That's a good one!" Sherman smiled. "Thanks, Carmen!"

"You're welcome," I said.

"What about me?" Miles asked. "What makes me unique?"

"Simple. It's your video skills. I bet you'll film Hollywood movies someday," I said.

"You really think so?"

I nodded. "Yep!"

So everybody else asked me what made them unique, too. It was easy coming up with ideas.

Colby wrote his own songs. Hope was an amazing photographer for our school newspaper, the *Benton Bluff Bloodhound*. Little kids loved Kori, probably because she was great with them since she had three younger siblings. And Davis was a pioneer reenactor.

"How come I didn't know that about you, Davis?" Sherman asked.

Davis shrugged. "Probably because you never asked."

"So what about you, Carmen?" Colby asked. "What makes you unique?"

"Well . . ." I began. But then I was stumped. I didn't have any problem thinking of things that made the others unique, but I couldn't seem to think of anything for me.

Davis finally said, "I got it! You volunteer at the humane society."

I was there every Saturday. That's where I adopted my cats, Stoffie and Mesa. But I wasn't so sure that was unique. I decided to just leave that line blank for now.

"And you really are a peacemaker, too," Miles added. "Just like Mr. Byrd said."

"That's Carmen for you," Hope said. "Always trying to get along with everybody."

That didn't seem like such a bad thing. But the way Hope said it, it sure sounded like it was.

"Some people are impossible to get along with," Davis said.

"Like Natalie," Hope added.

Uh-oh. Here they went.

"Exactly," Davis said.

I tried changing the subject. "Hey, do you guys remember the time—"

"Natalie looks way too comfortable sitting at Mr. Byrd's desk if you ask me," Davis said, cutting me off.

"I noticed that, too," Hope said. "And what's up with all of these worksheets?"

"They weren't that bad, though," I said. "It didn't take us too long to finish. Plus, we learned more about each other's instruments."

"And each other," Colby said.

"Puh-lease," Hope said. "Because of Natalie, we had zero practice in the band room today. And we haven't even started on selecting music for *What's Your Holiday?* We only have three weeks left until opening night, you know."

"We'll just have to work really hard to get ready," I said.

"I wonder why I wasn't selected to be on the committee," Davis said. Then he looked at Kori. "We've both been in this band longer than Carmen, Miles, and Colby. That's not fair."

Kori nodded. "I didn't want to say anything, but I sort of wondered that, too."

"If Mr. Byrd knew you liked Natalie better than you do him, I bet he wouldn't have picked you," Hope said to the three of us.

"I don't like Natalie better than Mr. Byrd," I said. "I like them both."

"Me too," Miles said.

Davis frowned. "Really?"

"Yeah," I said. "I've already learned a lot from Mr. Byrd, but Natalie is cool, too."

"And I like Mr. Byrd, but he can be a little tough sometimes," Colby said.

Davis's eyes widened. "Tough? That's just because he loves band so much, and he wants us

to know our stuff. Natalie probably doesn't know the difference between a quarter note and an eighth note," he said, getting louder.

"That's ridiculous. Of course she does!" Miles said even louder than Davis.

"Let's just forget it," I said. "I've been brainstorming some ideas for *What's Your Holiday?* We could work on that right now."

"No!" Miles and Hope shouted at the same time.

"Okeydokey," I said. "It was just an idea."

Rube headed toward our table then. "Whoo-wee! What's going on over here? You're as loud as any jazz band I ever heard. Except your voices sound angry."

Nobody said anything.

"You can tell me, or not. But when you've got a problem bottled up inside of you, just bustin' to get out," he punched the air, "it's better to talk about it. Listen to this old man. I know what I'm talking about."

Everybody was still quiet. But Rube was right. If we didn't talk about it, then people would stay mad. Or even get more mad, if that was possible.

"Rube," I finally said, "the Benton Bluff Junior High band is a band divided."

Chapter 5
A BAND DIVIDED

"A band divided, huh?" Rube said. "I'd like to hear more about that. Maybe there's a chance you can put your band back together again."

"I don't know about that," Davis grumbled. "Maybe we're like Humpty Dumpty."

"He couldn't be put back together again either," Hope said.

Then she and Davis changed where they were sitting around the table. It was like the old band kids were against us newer band kids. We were split in two groups!

Rube grabbed a chair from another table and pulled it over to ours. Except he didn't sit on either side. His chair was at one end, like he was the head of some business meeting. "Maybe you should start from the beginning," he said.

So Sherman began telling Rube all about Mr. Byrd's big student teacher announcement last week. "At first, Natalie just observed us," he said. "At least that's what she called it. But I'm pretty sure she's a secret spy. She even wheels her gear around in a rolling case everywhere she goes."

That was another thing about Sherman. Besides yo-yos, he was also big-time into spy flicks. So he had a way of making things seem much more top secret than they really were. By now, Rube knew that, too. He just smiled and said, "Go on."

"Today, Mr. Byrd let Natalie teach the class. But she didn't even teach us anything," Sherman said.

"Right!" Davis jumped in. "All she did was hand out a ton of worksheets. See?" He showed Rube his booklet to prove it.

Rube flipped through the stack of papers. "I do see," he said.

"I mean, whoever heard of band students coloring pictures of clarinets and trombones for an assignment, anyway?" Hope said.

"Not me," Rube said.

Davis looked across the table at us. "Even Rube is on our side," he said.

"Whoo-wee! Slow down there, Davis." Rube held up one hand. "I never said that."

"You've got to pick a side, though." Davis pointed to their side of the table first. "Right." Then he pointed to our side. "And wrong."

Colby must've thought that would make a perfect song because he started singing, "Right or wrong, I knew it all along."

Miles elbowed him. "Can you save your next hit for some other time? Rube is about to pick a side here."

"Sorry," Colby said.

"That's okay," Rube said. "And I'm not choosing anybody's side. That's called remaining neutral."

He smiled. "But I do want to hear more about this Natalie. What other terrible things has she done?"

I wasn't so sure that Rube hadn't really picked a side. He sure sounded as if he was on theirs.

Hope showed Rube the worksheet we had to fill out about ourselves. "This," she said.

"Hmm," Rube said, his forehead creasing in wrinkles. "That doesn't look so bad to me."

"The worst part is that they," Davis pointed toward us, "all like Natalie better than Mr. Byrd."

Rube looked at us. "Is this true?"

I shook my head. "No. We like them both."

"But Natalie's class is easier," Colby said. "It's sort of like we're getting a break for a few weeks while she's in the band room."

"There's nothing wrong with that." Rube smiled. "We could all use a little break every now and again. Right?"

Now Rube sounded more like he was on our side.

"Wrong!" Davis said. Then he told Rube all about Mr. Minotti, the student teacher he had back in fourth grade. "Thanks to him, my multiplication was all mixed up."

"Quick!" Rube said. "What's four times eight?"

"Thirty-two," Davis answered.

"Six times nine?" Rube quizzed him again.

"It's fifty-four. So what?"

"So you certainly know your facts now, Davis," Rube said.

Davis frowned. "I guess so, but that doesn't have anything to do with band."

"Do any of you know how I learned my multiplication tables?" Rube asked. "And don't you say by carving them on a stone tablet either." He slapped his knee and laughed.

"Tell us," I said.

"I learned my math facts by singing songs." And then Rube sang, "Two times two is four, and two times three is six."

Colby joined in. "Two times four is eight, and two times five is ten." He smiled. "I know that tune. It's 'Row, Row, Row Your Boat.'"

Rube snapped his fingers. "Bingo! You got it."

"That's another thing," Hope said. "Natalie made us play Band Bingo today."

"Was it fun?" Rube asked.

Davis shrugged. "Sort of."

"But band isn't supposed to be fun," Hope said.

Rube leaned back in his chair. "Huh. It isn't?"

Hope had to think about that for a minute. "Well, it is," she finally said. "But not all the time. It has to be serious, too, so we can learn stuff."

"Yeah, games might be fun. But my mom made me take an extra summer class to learn my multiplication tables. I promise, taking a summer class while your friends are swimming and riding bikes isn't so fun," Davis said.

"And besides," he added, "next year, I have to try out for the high school concert band. If all we do at band practice now is play bingo and color pictures, I'm afraid I won't be good enough."

Hope seemed to understand. "And I'm afraid I won't get a band scholarship to college, like my sister did," she said.

"Fear!" Rube said then. "Now we're really getting somewhere. Fear makes people behave in ways they wouldn't ordinarily behave. Like dividing up bands."

I glanced across the table at Davis. He looked at me then, too. We were used to working together in the percussion section every day. And now, I was pretty sure we couldn't keep a beat together if we had to. How did things even turn into this?

Nobody said anything for a few moments. Then Rube finally said, "I want to show you kids something." He stood up and headed toward the front counter. Then he looked back over his shoulder at us. "Don't just sit there. Are you coming or not?"

So we all followed Rube to the front of the store. When everyone was gathered around, Rube whistled and called, "Mel!"

A few seconds later, Rube's old dog trotted out from behind the counter. She was black with graying paws and ears. Mel was a weird name for a girl, but Rube just called her that for short. Her real name was Melody.

"Say hello to the kids, Mel," Rube told her.

"Hey, Mel." I reached down to pet her.

She wagged her tail. And when Mel had gotten a pat from all of us, Rube said, "Now here's what I want to show you." He pointed his finger. "Mel, cork grease!"

Mel took off down one of the aisles. It wasn't long until she came back with a tube of cork grease in her mouth.

"Wow! How'd she do that?" I asked.

Rube held up one finger. "Wait. She's not done yet. Mel," he pointed again, "reeds!"

"She'll never get this," Davis said.

But a couple of minutes later, sure enough, Mel trotted back over carrying a box of reeds.

"No way!" Hope said.

"That's awesome!" Miles said. "I've got to film Mel sometime."

Rube took the box from Mel's mouth and gave her a treat. "Yes, siree. I think she'd like starring

in one of your videos, Miles." He scratched Mel's ears. "Wouldn't you, girl?"

"I've been teaching tricks to some of the dogs at the shelter. It makes them more adoptable. Maybe you could give me some pointers," I said.

"I'd be glad to," Rube said. "Any time."

"Cool! Thanks!"

"You're welcome, Carmen." Rube smiled. "But here's what I wanted to show you kids. See, Melody's an old dog, but this old man still taught her some new tricks. You kids aren't old dogs." He laughed then. "Whoo-wee! You're young pups yet. And your fresh minds can learn new tricks, too. It doesn't matter if the teacher is new, too. Do you understand?"

I thought I did. "Basically, you're saying we can learn new stuff, and we can learn it in different ways. Even from a new teacher, like Natalie. Right?"

"Smart girl." Rube winked. "Now if you'll excuse me, I have a customer waiting."

When you argue with somebody, it gets sort of awkward at first when you don't know what to say to make things right again. We all sort of stood around, like nobody was sure what to do. Luckily, Colby broke the silence then with another of his silly made-up songs about dogs in a band. That got everybody laughing.

And we laughed again when Davis joked, "Hey, the next time we come to Jazz Front, I bet Mel will be working the cash register."

But when everybody stopped laughing, I got serious for a second. "Are we okay again, guys?"

"Of course we're okay," Davis said. "Well, except Colby. We're not sure about him yet."

"Hey!" Colby grinned.

It felt really good to joke around and have things back to normal. Hopefully everything would stay that way.

Chapter 6

STOP & LISTEN

For the next few days, everything in room 217 stayed on track, even with Natalie leading our band practice. We spent our entire class in the library on Tuesday, so we could research a band-related topic that interested us. On Wednesday, we wrote two-page papers based on our research. Then everyone shared their reports with the rest of the band on Thursday.

Natalie's teaching style was still totally different from Mr. Byrd's. We hadn't actually, you know, practiced with our instruments since she'd taken over our class. But nobody really complained.

At least, nobody complained until Friday. That's when Natalie's newest lesson plan might've been her weirdest one yet.

"To kick off our weekend, I thought we'd do something extra fun today," Natalie said.

"More coloring sheets, *mademoiselle*?" Lem asked.

Natalie smiled. "Not this time, Lem."

"If it's bingo again," Davis whispered, "I'm out of here."

"Today, we're going to do something very interactive." Natalie held up a small notepad. "You're going to be musical detectives! Isn't that exciting?"

Davis slid all the way down in his seat. "I can't take much more of this," he complained.

"Let me explain how this works. You'll each get your own notepad, and I want you to investigate the sounds in your world. For example, listen."

Natalie cupped one hand behind her ear. Then she said, "Tick, tick, tick, tick," and nodded her head in time with the clock hanging on the wall. "Even the clock has its own beat. If you don't stop to listen, you'll miss out on the music that's all around you."

"So what's the notepad for?" Sherman asked.

Natalie smiled again. "That is where you'll record your findings. Your assignment is to write down the sound you hear, where you heard the sound, and how the sound makes you feel. So grab a pencil and come get a notepad. Mr. Byrd, I have one for you, too."

"Thank you, Natalie," he said, heading up front with the rest of us. Mr. Byrd hadn't said much since Natalie had taken over our class. I wondered what he really thought about how band practice was going.

When everyone had a notepad, Natalie said, "Go investigate to see what music you can find right here in the band room."

Everyone scrambled around the room. Sherman headed toward the lockers where we kept our instruments when we weren't using them.

"I can find a lot of music right here," he said, tugging on his locker.

Natalie laughed. "I don't think so, Sherman. Be sure it isn't an actual musical instrument, everyone. Really think outside the box."

"Got any ideas, Carmen?" Colby asked.

"Not yet." I scanned the room. What made it even worse was that the whole band scrambled around the room, searching for different sounds. It was hard to see anything that might be good to list. "This isn't as easy as I thought it would be."

"Tell me about it," Colby said.

"Watch it, lovebirds. I'm coming through," Davis said, squeezing between Colby and me. He knocked my notepad right out of my hand. "Oops! Sorry, Carmen!" Davis handed it back to me and took off.

"Did you hear that?" I asked Colby.

Colby nodded. "Yeah, just ignore Davis. He makes dumb jokes sometimes."

He must've thought I was talking about Davis calling us lovebirds just now, which totally was a dumb joke. Talk about embarrassing! And *so* not true. At least, I didn't think it was. Anyway, that didn't matter right now.

"I'm not talking about his joke." I smiled. "I meant did you hear the sound Davis made when he accidentally knocked the notepad out of my hand?" Then I dropped my notepad on purpose to recreate the sound.

"Do that again," Colby said.

So I dropped it several times in a row, and Colby snapped his fingers. "Hey, that does make a beat."

"It's music," I said, jotting down that sound on my notepad.

"Don't forget to add how the sound makes you feel."

"Right." I thought about it for a second before writing *Rushed.*

"Why rushed?" Colby asked.

"Because if I was heading to class and dropped my notebook, I'd feel rushed to pick it up if I'm in a hurry," I explained.

Colby smiled. "That makes sense."

"C'mon, let's see what else we can find," I said.

We looked behind Mr. Byrd's desk, over by the trophy case, and all around our chairs. And so far, we'd added a big fat nothing to our notepads. Natalie didn't say how many things we had to find, so maybe she'd settle for one.

I sat down in one of the chairs and closed my eyes, trying to think of something else to list. Then it hit me. "Colby! I know what we're doing wrong."

"Uh, what?" he said.

"Sit down." I patted the seat beside me. "Now close your eyes."

"Okay, now I really can't hear anything with everyone's shoes stomping across the floor. And somebody keeps coughing," Colby said.

I opened my eyes and nodded. "Exactly! All that stuff is music. We couldn't find anything because we were looking for stuff. But music is listening."

"Hey, that's pretty smart, Carmen!" He held his hand up for a high five.

After that, we didn't have any problem filling up our notepads. While everyone else ran around the room, Colby and I sat there listening for all of the sounds around us. Before class was over, I added all sorts of things, like a zipping purse, change jingling in someone's pocket, and somebody walking past clicking a mechanical pencil.

I even knew when Natalie headed toward us because I heard her boot heels clicking across the floor. "Carmen, Colby, is something wrong? You two aren't bustling around like everyone else is for this assignment."

"That's because we're working smarter," Colby said.

"Tell me more," Natalie said.

So Colby told her all about how we had walked around looking for stuff, and we stunk at it. "But then Carmen got the idea to sit here, and you know, just listen. And we got tons of ideas." He held up his notepad to show her.

"Carmen!" Natalie gushed. "I'm super impressed by your insight. In fact, both of you have made some keen observations."

Colby brought out his air guitar and rocked to his newest made-up tune. "Teacher says I'm keen, but what's that even mean?"

Natalie smiled and shook her head. Then she said, "Class, I'd like to share how Carmen and Colby approached this assignment." After she finished telling them how we'd stopped to listen for the sounds around us, she said, "Well done, musical detectives! I'm proud of you both."

Mr. Byrd came over then and patted us on the shoulder. "Good going, guys! And great activity, Natalie."

Natalie told him. "My minor is in theater, and it's an exercise we learned onstage, except I modified it for the band room."

"I think it was a hit. And speaking of theater," Mr. Byrd looked at Colby and me, "time is running out until opening night of *What's Your Holiday?* How are those plans coming along, so we can work on it as a group?"

I wanted to say, "Plans? What plans?" Because so far, I couldn't get everyone on board to work on the project. I had brainstormed some ideas on my own, but they probably weren't very good.

I didn't want to tell Mr. Byrd any of that, though. He really was one of my favorite teachers, even if Davis didn't believe that. And I knew Mr. Byrd was counting on the theater committee to come through.

"I think we'll have something to run by you on Monday," I said. Okay, so that wasn't totally true. But it wasn't a lie, either. Did the committee have anything planned now? No! But I had all weekend to get everyone together to put our musical score together for the show.

Mr. Byrd smiled. "That sounds perfect! Thank you, Carmen."

"No problem!" I smiled back.

Then Natalie asked him to sign some forms she needed to submit to her college professor, and they headed toward Mr. Byrd's desk. I let out a huge sigh.

I started putting my things into my backpack before the bell rang. Then Davis and Hope walked over. They stopped right in front of Colby and me.

"Hey, Hope!" He sniffed the air. "Do you smell something?"

Hope pretended to sniff too. "Yeah, it smells funky to me. What is it?"

He pointed at Colby and me. "Oh, I get it. It's teacher's pets." Then he pinched his nose.

"*Student* teacher's pets," Hope said. She pinched her nose, too, and imitated Natalie with, "Well done! I'm soooo proud of you both!"

Uh-oh. I told Mr. Byrd it would be no problem for the theater committee to have plans ready to run by him on Monday. Now I wasn't so sure. It might be a problem after all. A *big* problem.

Chapter 7

HOLIDAY PLANS

"Are you sure Miles's mom doesn't mind you kids meeting at their house today?" my dad asked on the way over there the next day. "It is a bit last-minute."

It was Saturday, and I had texted everyone on the theater committee earlier to see about getting together this afternoon.

"Meeting at Miles's house was his idea, so I'm sure his mom is cool with it," I said.

Dad hit his turn signal and pulled into Creekwood Court, the subdivision where Miles lived. The closer to his house we got, the more flippity-floppity my stomach got.

Dad noticed. "Are you okay, Carmen? Let me turn down the heat," he said, reaching for the dial.

"No, I'm good. It's just, after what happened with Hope and Davis yesterday, I really don't feel up to working on *What's Your Holiday?* this weekend. I mean, I really, really don't feel up to it. But I sort of promised Mr. Byrd the committee would have plans ready to share with him on Monday, so I don't have a choice.

"Gotcha," Dad said. "Just remember, you're new to the band this year, so you're already used to change. Some of the older members have been there for a while, and that could have a lot to do with their reaction to Natalie. Change can be scary for some people."

"Yeah, and change can make some people act plain scary," I joked.

Dad laughed. "That's true, too, I suppose."

Even though we were laughing now, I didn't feel like laughing yesterday when Colby and I had been called teacher's pets. But what Dad said just now about change being scary made sense.

"If you don't want to go, you can always change your mind," Dad said. "I can turn the car around."

Turning around and heading back home sounded easy. And safer than meeting up with Hope again today. But I'd already put a lot of time into the project on my own.

Besides, Monday was only two days away, and our theater committee had to have a plan ready for Mr. Byrd. That way we'd still have a couple of weeks left to practice our musical score for the show. Plus, it probably wouldn't be as bad meeting with just Hope. Davis wasn't even on the theater committee.

I decided I didn't feel like playing it safe today. "Thanks, Dad," I finally said. "But I can do this."

When Dad dropped me off at Miles's house, Sherman and Colby were already there. Now we were just waiting for Hope to show up. A few minutes later, she did. But it wasn't just Hope at the door.

"Guess who tagged along?" Davis said, plopping onto a couch cushion in Miles's family room where we'd planned to have our meeting.

"But you're not on the committee," Colby said.

Hope nodded. "He's not officially, but I figured we could use more help. And I didn't think anyone would mind," she said, looking at me.

"Sure, that's cool," I said. Honestly, I did kind of mind. I mean, Mr. Byrd didn't select Davis for the committee like he did the rest of us. But we only had a couple of hours to work, and it definitely wasn't worth wasting any more time arguing.

"Haven't you already been working on some ideas, Carmen?" Colby asked.

"Yep, I did a lot of research. That way we can understand the different holidays we're creating a score for." I opened the folder I brought with me.

"Whoa!" Miles said. "That is a lot of work."

I guess I had done a lot. But reading through the script and adding music and sound to the places where Mrs. Dillingham, the theater director, had suggested turned out to be a lot of fun. I actually liked working on this project.

"But is it any good?" Hope asked, reaching for my notes. She started reading aloud. "Hanukkah, or the Festival of Lights, lasts for eight days and nights. Families light the menorah, eat latkes, or potato pancakes, and play the dreidel game."

"Wait, what's a dreidel?" Sherman asked.

"Picture a four-sided spinning top," I said.

Miles wheeled over to get his laptop. A few seconds later he said, "Here it is. This website says there's a Hebrew letter on each side."

Everyone gathered around to see. "That's pretty cool," Colby said.

"Next is Ramadan," Hope went on.

"I remember that holiday," Miles said. "It's the Muslim holy month."

Hope held one finger up to her lips. "Shhh, I'm reading. Anyway," she continued, "Muslims fast.

That means they don't eat or drink anything, not even water, from dawn to sunset every day during Ramadan. The celebration ends with Eid al-Fitr, or the Festival of Breaking the Fast. After special prayers and a sermon, families visit each other's homes to have meals together."

"Christmas is next," Davis said, reading over Hope's shoulder.

Hope cleared her throat and read, "Christians celebrate the birth of Jesus Christ each year on December 25. Families decorate with Christmas trees and lights. They also sing songs, exchange special gifts, and share meals together."

Sherman patted his stomach. "Yummy! I like the holidays with meals."

Everybody laughed until Hope shushed us all again.

"The last holiday is Kwanzaa, or 'first fruits,' in Swahili," she said. "For seven days each December, African Americans celebrate their African heritage.

Families light a new candle on the kinara each evening. On the last day, families often exchange handmade gifts." Hope flipped to the next page and ended with, "African drums beat a rhythm for songs and dancing at celebrations."

"Well, we'll need drums for that part." Colby went into air-drummer mode. Everyone joined in playing pretend drums. I guess even Hope couldn't resist because she joined in, too. The longer we played, the more into it we got. That is, until Miles's mom brought us some snacks.

"I thought you might be hungry," she said, placing a tray of fruit and veggies on the coffee table and trying not to laugh.

Davis grabbed a carrot stick and said, "Thank you, Mrs. Darr!"

She smiled. "You're welcome. Let me know if you need anything else."

"Sure, Mom," Miles said. "Thanks!"

I reached for a kiwi slice, and said, "So what

did you guys think about my notes?"

"Everything sounded good to me," Colby said.

"Like that's a surprise," Davis said.

Miles wiped his mouth on a napkin. "Hey, I thought it sounded good, too."

Hope shrugged. "It was okay, I guess."

When she wasn't looking, Colby stuck his tongue out at her. It was all I could do to keep from choking on a strawberry.

Anyway, I ignored Hope. We still had work to do. I grabbed my folder and pulled out the *What's Your Holiday?* script. "Mrs. Dillingham made notes for places to add some songs. Does anyone have any suggestions?"

Miles logged back onto the Internet, and we spent some time researching different songs. Nobody seemed to agree. Colby wanted something fun and upbeat. Miles wanted a song that spotlighted the brass section. Then Hope and Sherman said that focusing more on flute solos would sound better for holiday tunes.

"Since we only have a couple of weeks left to practice before opening night, maybe we should choose music that we can learn easily," I suggested.

Hope frowned. "Did I miss something here? I don't remember Mr. Byrd appointing you as the theater committee leader, or anything."

"Right, he didn't. I'm just trying to help," I said.

"More like trying to take over," Hope said. "You're just like your favorite teacher, Natalie."

Not this again.

"Okay, forget choosing sheet music for now," I said. "Mrs. Dillingham also made notes in the script for places where she wanted us to make different sounds. Do you guys want to work on that?"

Miles nodded. "I do. This Kwanzaa scene says a festive sound is needed as gifts are exchanged. But what sound should we add there?"

"I'm not sure. But I think instead of looking for different sounds, we should listen until we find the right one," Colby said. "It sort of reminds me of the musical detectives exercise we did in class yesterday."

"Puh-lease," Hope said. "That was one of the worst lessons ever. Didn't you think so, Sherman?"

Sherman's curly hair boinged up and down when he nodded.

Hope glanced at Davis. "What about you?"

"Yep," Davis said, chomping celery.

That's all it took to get another argument going. The entire rest of the time, instead of working on our theater production, Hope, Davis, and Sherman bashed Natalie's class. It was like the old band members versus the new ones.

The way I saw it, nobody won. By the time we left Miles's house, we still didn't have any real details to share with Mr. Byrd. How could I tell him that on Monday?

Chapter 8

TAKING CREDIT

"Maybe Mr. Byrd will forget we're supposed to discuss our score for *What's Your Holiday?*" I said to Colby and Miles on Monday in the band room.

"No way!" Miles said. "Mr. Byrd doesn't forget anything. Ever."

And when Mr. Byrd made his way to the front of the band room, I had a feeling Miles was right about that.

"Before class gets underway, I'd like to call the theater committee together for a quick meeting," he said.

Miles glanced my way. "Told you!"

Yeah, he told me all right. But what in the world would I tell Mr. Byrd?

When our group was up front, Mr. Byrd smiled and rubbed his hands together. "I've been excited all weekend to see what you guys came up with for the theater production," he said.

Nobody said anything.

"Who wants to start?" Mr. Byrd went on.

Crickets.

"Anyone?" he asked.

Still silence.

"Okay, then." Mr. Byrd folded his arms across his chest. "When I selected you all for this committee, I did so expecting you'd have tons of ideas for us to work with. Has coming up with something been that difficult?"

Coming up with ideas wasn't the difficult part. It was working with Hope and Sherman that was so hard. And when they brought Davis into it, forget it. Working together was impossible.

I had to tell Mr. Byrd. But before I could speak up, Hope beat me to it.

"So far, we've done a ton of research on the different holidays," she said.

We had done a ton of research? That was funny. Because the whole time *I* was searching online and reading books and making notes about the different holidays, Hope wasn't around. And neither was anyone else.

"Did you know that the mkeka is a straw or cloth mat placed at the center of the table during Kwanzaa?" Hope went on.

Mr. Byrd shook his head. "No, I didn't."

"It symbolizes African history," she said, "and other Kwanzaa symbols are placed on or near it."

"Very good, Hope!" Mr. Byrd said.

Yeah, it was good. And it came straight from my notes. The nerve of that girl!

Colby knew it, too. He started to speak up. "Hey, wait a minute—"

"We've all learned a lot," Hope said, cutting off Colby. The look on her face practically dared

anyone to say anything different. "But because we've spent so much time on the research part, we haven't spent as much time creating the score. Can we have a few more days to work?"

Mr. Byrd looked at me then.

"I thought we could have it ready by today, sir, but we just couldn't get it together. I'm sorry," I said.

"That's fine." Mr. Byrd smiled. "I understand it was a big task, and I'm proud of you all for your hard work so far. Just a moment, let me check my calendar." He stepped away.

"Are you kidding me?" Colby said as soon as Mr. Byrd was out of earshot. "You know that research was all Carmen's."

Hope shrugged. "It's a group effort, right? And once Carmen shared it with the group on Saturday, it became all of our work."

"But you're taking all of the credit," Miles jumped in. "That's not fair."

"It's no biggie," I said.

But the expression on my face must've given away that it was a biggie. When Mr. Byrd came back with his calendar, he looked puzzled. "Is everything okay?"

"Sure," I said, smiling. "Everything is great."

Mr. Byrd didn't look like he totally bought it. "If there's any sort of problem, I'd like to know about it." Nobody spoke up, so he pointed to Thursday on his calendar. "This is the day that our band is scheduled to practice at the community center with the *What's Your Holiday?* cast. We need to be there from six o'clock until eight o'clock."

I leaned in for a better look. "Are we practicing the same time on Friday and Saturday, too?" I asked.

"Yes," Mr. Byrd said. "And next week, we'll practice Monday, Tuesday, and Thursday, giving us six practices total before the opening that Friday. So," he looked at us, "if you five can get the score turned in by this Thursday, we should be all set."

Hope smiled. "You can count on us, Mr. Byrd."

Then Mrs. Goble, our school secretary, called Mr. Byrd to the office.

"I know I can count on you," Mr. Byrd said before heading toward the door. "That's why I chose you for this project."

Yeah, I was starting to think choosing us was a mistake. A big one. We just couldn't seem to work together. And after class, I found out that some people on the committee didn't even want to try working together anymore.

Miles, Colby, and I were deciding when we could have another committee meeting when Hope came over. Sherman and Davis were with her, too.

"We need to talk," Hope said, looking serious.

"Okay," I said. "We're listening."

"Mr. Byrd is counting on us to work out the details for the *What's Your Holiday?* score, and none of us want to let him down," she began.

I nodded. "That's something we all agree on."

"The problem is, we just don't work well together," Hope said. "I think we should split up."

"What do you mean?" Miles asked.

"You know," Davis said, putting his hands together and then stretching them as far apart as he could, "you do your thing, and we'll do ours."

"Wait, do you keep forgetting you're not even on this committee, Davis?" Colby asked.

"Mr. Byrd won't mind. Anyway, there's three of you," he pointed to Miles, Colby, and me, "and there's three of us." He pointed to himself, Hope, and Sherman. "That makes it even."

"And to make everything else even, we'll split the work. You take this part," Hope said, handing us half of the script.

"Let me get this straight," I said. "On Thursday, you want us to give Mr. Byrd the score for Kwanzaa and Ramadan? And you're going to turn in the score for Christmas and Hanukkah?"

"You got it," Hope said, whirling around. And they took off.

I looked at Colby and Miles. "I don't think we're a band divided anymore," I said.

"We're not?" Miles asked.

"Nope," I said, holding up our half of the script. "I think we're officially a band divorced."

For the next few days, Miles, Colby, and I met in the school library each day after school to work on our half of the musical score. On Thursday, we were ready to share our work with Mr. Byrd.

"I wasn't so sure about it at first, but Hope's idea to split up into two groups actually worked," I said at band practice.

"Agreed!" Miles said. "Our score for Ramadan and Kwanzaa is perfect, if you ask me."

Colby nodded. "I just wonder what their group came up with for Hanukkah and Christmas."

"I don't know," I said. "But we'll find out as soon as Mr. Byrd gets here."

The only problem was that Mr. Byrd never got to room 217. As in, band practice was almost over, and Mr. Byrd was a no-show.

"I hope you're happy now," Hope said to me before the bell rang. "Even Mr. Byrd has had enough of Natalie's terrible lessons." She wiped her hands on her jeans. "I can't believe she's turned band practice into art class."

Today, Natalie's lesson was Musical December. She showed us videos of people from all different cultures ringing in the holidays with music.

After that, she had us glitter-fy a music note hanging from a star. She said it was for us all to remember that no matter what, we're musical stars. Maybe it was a little corny, but I hadn't cut and glued in forever. So it was sort of fun, too.

Anyway, I didn't know why Mr. Byrd wasn't here, but I was pretty sure it had nothing to do with Natalie. To prove it, I decided to ask Natalie if she knew.

"Yes, Carmen?" Natalie said when she noticed my hand raised.

"I'm just wondering, where is Mr. Byrd?"

Natalie snapped her fingers. "I almost forgot." She reached into her pocket and pulled out a note. "Thanks for reminding me, Carmen. This is from Mr. Byrd." She read:

Dear Class,

I'm sorry to leave on such short notice, but I am attending a school band directors' conference in South Carolina. Listen to Natalie while I'm away. I'll see you next week!

Mr. Byrd

"Next week?" Hope grumbled. "Mr. Byrd's gone, and Natalie's completely in charge for a whole week. I hope you're happy!"

Chapter 9
IN THE SILENCE

"Whatever," I said to Hope. "Mr. Byrd'll still be back in time for *What's Your Holiday?* next week." That reminded me. "Do you guys have your part ready to practice tonight?"

Hope stared down at her feet like she'd just discovered they existed. "About that . . ." she finally said. "We're not ready."

"No way!" I said, hoping she was kidding

"It's not my fault," Hope began. "Sherman got sick. And Davis wasn't much help."

I bet Mr. Byrd knew Davis wouldn't be. That's probably why he wasn't picked in the first place.

"And I've been practicing my flute extra, extra hard at home," Hope went on. "I've got to get a music scholarship for college, you know."

What were we going to do? Our musical score wasn't completely ready, and we only had four hours until we had to be at the community center to practice with the cast. Not only were we a band divided and divorced, we were a band disaster!

I started to panic a little. We'd look like total losers in front of everyone tonight. Then I got an idea.

"So you're probably wondering why I asked you here early," I said after school that afternoon. I'd asked everyone on the theater committee to meet at the community center where *What's Your Holiday?* would be performed next week. I'd even asked Davis, since he'd managed to crash all of the other meetings anyway. "Somehow, we're going to finish the score, just as Mr. Byrd expects."

Miles and Colby clapped, and I felt my cheeks heat up.

"Don't worry, we're not doing this alone. I asked for help." I pointed toward our helper, who had just arrived.

"Natalie!" Hope groaned.

"That's right." I motioned her over to our corner table in the lobby. "I didn't think you'd mind." I gave Hope the same line she'd given the rest of the committee when she invited Davis to our meeting.

Davis frowned. "Like she'll be any help. No telling what lame ideas she'll come up with."

I knew Natalie overheard what Davis just said. I mean, as loud as he said it, how could she not?

"That was mean," I said. "You guys have had it in for Natalie since she first walked into the band room, and for no good reason." It felt good to take a stand.

"It's okay, Carmen," Natalie said, sliding into a seat beside me. "I could sense that some people didn't like my lesson plans each day as well as others did. And that's okay. Teaching is sort of like band. You guys learn what techniques work for you, and which ones don't. I've been learning for the past few weeks which teaching techniques work for me, and which ones aren't so hot."

She smiled and glanced at Hope, Davis, and Sherman. "I've enjoyed my time in the band room with you. With all of you. And I'm sorry if you've been miserable the last few weeks."

I saw Hope squirming in her chair. "I guess I haven't been totally fair," she finally said.

"You think?" Miles asked.

"Yeah, me neither," Sherman admitted, too.

Everyone looked at Davis. "Fine, I guess I've been a jerk lately," he finally said.

"I promise I don't normally act like such a brat," Hope said. "It's just hit me with all of the studying I've been doing for tests before winter break that the school year is almost halfway over already."

"Pretty soon we'll be graduating from eighth grade, and then it's high school," Sherman added.

Davis looked really sad when he said, "And then we'll leave the Benton Bluff Junior High band room and Mr. Byrd."

"Forever," Hope finished.

"And you guys probably didn't expect a student teacher to come along and horn in on the time you have with Mr. Byrd, huh?" Natalie said softly.

Hope shook her head. "I'm really going to miss him next year."

"Me too," Davis said.

I guess Dad was right when he said change was scary for some people. Heading to high school next year would mean a ton of changes for Hope, Davis, and Sherman. Some scary changes.

Even though it hadn't been easy to get along with those three lately, now it made sense why they didn't want a student teacher around. I got it. If it were me, I'd probably feel the same way. I sort of felt sorry for them.

"So anyway," Hope said then, "I'm really sorry."

Davis swallowed hard. "Yeah, me too."

"We all are," Sherman said.

Natalie smiled. "It's okay. Really." Then she held out her hand to them. "Truce?"

"Truce!" Hope, Davis, and Sherman agreed, taking turns shaking Natalie's hand.

"Awesome!" Natalie glanced at her watch. "But what isn't so awesome is that we have two hours to finish the score for the production. Carmen, please tell us what you have in mind."

I pulled out the folder I'd brought with all of my notes inside. "So Miles, Colby, and I have the score finished for the part of the play about Ramadan and Kwanzaa. Since you're also studying theater, what do you think?" I asked, handing it to Natalie.

"You're majoring in theater, too?" Hope asked.

"Actually, theater is my minor. I was undecided between teaching music and teaching theater. I love them both, but music, as you can see, eventually won out," Natalie explained.

"Man," Davis said, "if you're studying music and theater, then our score should be epic."

Natalie smiled. "Except this score is your work. I'm only here for backup, if needed. And from what I've seen so far," Natalie handed the paper back to me, "this looks fantastic. So what ideas do you have for Hanukkah and Christmas?"

"I brought along some sheet music," I said. "I thought maybe we should play songs that most people know, but we should also keep it fairly simple since we're only getting in six practices before showtime."

"That seems like a smart idea," Natalie agreed, looking over the music, and everyone nodded.

Next we moved on to discussing some of the sounds scattered throughout the scenes.

"Look at the Hanukkah scene," I said. "The lines here are light, so an instrument that plays light tones would work perfectly here."

"Like a flute?" Hope asked.

I nodded. "That's what I had in mind."

"I can play a solo," Sherman volunteered.

Hope shook her head. "I don't think so!"

"But I want to play it," Sherman argued.

And Hope shot back, "So do I!"

Maybe Mr. Byrd was right about that whole peacemaker thing. The way Hope and Sherman acted right now, we definitely needed one.

"Here's an idea," I said. "The auditorium is pretty big. If there's only one flutist playing, the sound might get lost in there. Why don't you play a duet?"

"Good call, Carmen," Natalie said. "I noticed on that worksheet I gave you a few weeks ago, you didn't tell me something that makes you unique. Maybe it's sound design. You have a knack for it."

"Thanks!" I said. I really did like this project a lot. And now Hope and Sherman were both happy, and a duet actually worked best for our score. Double win!

We still had a few more details to work out. I suggested Miles would blow into his trumpet mouthpiece to make a car engine sound as families arrived in scenes for both Christmas and Hanukkah.

We used the listening exercise Natalie had taught us to choose a few common sounds to add to some scenes. Colby thought of crunching up potato chips to mimic a roaring fire in one scene where children hung stockings by a fireplace.

"That's perfect, Colby!" I said, giving him a high five.

Natalie checked the time again. "It's nearly practice time," she said. "You only need one more sound for the lighting of the menorah scene."

"How about a flute?" Sherman said.

I shook my head. "We're already using a scene with flutes. Let's do something different," I said. Then I closed my eyes and pictured a candle's flame. It slowly flickered back and forth, never making a sound. "I know! Silence."

"Silence? Is that a sound?" Miles asked.

Natalie nodded. "It sure is, Miles. In fact, actors use silence as a tool quite often with the timing of their lines and actions. In this instance of lighting the menorah, I think silence works beautifully."

"You're good at this, Carmen," Miles said. "Maybe you can help me select the sound for my videos some time."

"You've got it!" I smiled.

By then, Lem, Kori, and a lot of the other band kids were showing up to practice. And a lady with a floppy hat, dangly earrings, and bright red lipstick came over to our table. She had to be the director.

"Hello! I'm Mrs. Dillingham," she said grandly. "You must be the Benton Bluff Junior High band."

"Yes, ma'am, we are. I'm Natalie Tate, and I'll be filling in for Mr. Byrd."

"Mr. Byrd told me he was leaving the band in excellent hands. Are you ready to join us for practice?" Mrs. Dillingham asked.

Natalie looked around at the rest of us. "Ready, band?"

"Ready!" we all said.

In the last few weeks, sometimes I wondered if we'd ever have the musical score finished in time to accompany the theatrical production. But we actually did it. And it turned out pretty awesome. I could hardly wait for Mr. Byrd to get back from his conference, so he could hear it, too.

Chapter 10
THE BIG DEBUT

Our first practice with the theater production went pretty well. I mean, there were a few kinks. But hey, it was our band's first time playing with a cast of actors and actresses.

Mr. Byrd flew back from his band directors' conference to Benton Bluff the next week on Thursday, just a day before the first show. We begged him to come to practice with us that night for a sneak preview. But he said he wanted to be surprised.

Suddenly it was Friday. Opening night! And I was nervous. Sherman must've been nervous, too. He was always bouncing around, but tonight, he was practically bouncing into the rafters high overhead.

It didn't help backstage when Davis peeked from behind the curtain and said, "Wow! There are thousands of people out there."

Mr. Byrd smiled. "Davis, the theater only seats 800 people."

"Yeah, and that's almost a thousand," Davis said.

"Almost," Mr. Byrd agreed.

Natalie went around giving everyone last minute instructions. "Remember to stand up nice and tall. And be sure your shirts are tucked in."

"Speaking of shirts," Zac said, "I'm digging Mr. Byrd's."

His shirt must've been new. It was pretty tame for a Mr. Byrd shirt. Peaceful white clouds drifted on a blue background.

"You like?" Mr. Byrd asked. "The conference center was only about an hour's drive from the beach, so one afternoon I drove out to the shore."

"You mean, you finally made it to the beach?"

Lem said. "It's about time, *monsieur.*"

Mr. Byrd smiled, and Mrs. Dillingham came over then, packing a clipboard. "Showtime's in five minutes," she said all singsongy. "Places, everyone."

Beads of sweat popped up on my palms, and I didn't feel so great. I whispered to Colby beside me, "I can't do this."

"What?" He looked like I'd totally lost it. "I know you can do it, Carmen." Then he reached toward my hair. "Your flower's all crooked. Let me straighten it."

I stood perfectly still.

"How come you wear a flower in your hair every day?" Colby asked.

"Sometimes when I feel all daydreamy, I wear a daisy. Or if I'm sad, I wear a blue forget-me-not." I shrugged. "I just like flowers, I guess."

"Me too," Colby said. "I mean, I like them in your hair. It's cute."

I was glad the theater was dimly lit, so Colby couldn't see that my steaming cheeks probably matched the flower tucked behind my ear.

"So why'd you wear a red rose tonight?" Colby asked.

"Because red is a strong color, and I needed some extra courage to get up in front of all of these people. I mean, I'm a drummer." I bit my lip. "And I'm used to standing in the back of the band."

Colby nodded. "But tonight, there's no hiding in the back."

"Exactly," I said. "But this red rose is so not giving me a courage vibe."

See, at our first practice with the theater cast, Natalie asked me to help her lead the band instead of playing my snare drum since I'd basically written the entire score on my own. I thought it was just for that night. Wrong! She wanted me to help her at all of the other practices and tonight's performance, too.

"Carmen," Colby went on, "look at how you stood up for what you thought was right with Hope and Davis and Sherman. And you headed up the theater committee to put this musical score together. Trust me, you don't need a flower. You're already brave."

"You really think so?" I asked. I mean, I was usually pretty shy. I hadn't noticed it until now, but lately I hadn't been as much. At least, not in band.

Colby smiled. "Definitely!"

I hoped he was right. Either way, there was no backing out now. Our band took our place onstage. Mrs. Dillingham placed us toward the front, but just to the side of the set.

"Play like the musicians you are, band," Mr. Byrd whispered.

"Wait, where are you going?" I asked.

"To grab my seat and enjoy the performance. Natalie's got this, and so do you." He gave us a thumbs-up before disappearing into the darkness.

After that, the velvety blue curtains parted. The show kicked off with children parading across the stage. The brightly colored costumes they wore represented different cultures.

Then the spotlight shone on the narrator as he said, "The season was busy as families celebrated the holidays. But some families took time out to celebrate something else—diversity in others. Perhaps there are no greater gifts than simply being understood and accepted." He paused before asking, "What's your holiday?"

The spotlight flashed to center stage. For the first act, a family dusted off their Kwanzaa kinara for candle lighting. Just like we'd practiced, Miles buzzed into the mouthpiece of his trumpet to simulate a car engine sound. Then the family greeted friends as they arrived to join in the Kwanzaa celebration. As the scene progressed, the audience learned about the seven principles from *umoja*, or "unity," to *imani*, which meant "faith."

Once the scene ended, the curtains closed for a quick set change and reopened for a new scene—Ramadan. A Muslim family arose early for Suhoor, a predawn breakfast. Then they fasted all day before eating things like fruit and dates at the end of the day during the Iftar meal. That scene closed with a joyous Eid al-Fitr celebration.

Another set change set the scene for a family returning home from Christmas Eve church services. Then Colby, Zac, and Kori smashed bags of chips near the microphone to create the sound of a roaring fire as children hung stockings on the mantel. Our band played "We Wish You a Merry Christmas" as the scene ended.

After the very last set change, our band played another song, "Oh Hanukkah." Later, Hope and Sherman performed their flute duet together as children played a dreidel game and enjoyed *sufganiyot*, or donuts. The scene concluded with the lighting of the menorah.

I was especially nervous because this is where I'd suggested we cut the music and go for something completely different—silence. The entire auditorium fell quiet as the candles' flames flickered on stage. It was probably one of my favorite moments of the entire show. And I couldn't keep from smiling when Natalie leaned over and whispered, "That was lovely, Carmen."

The children who launched the show came back onto the stage once more to sing songs that celebrated each of the different holidays. The audience clapped as the curtains closed one last time, signaling the show's end. Backstage, all of the cast and crew cheered.

"What a success!" Natalie said.

I nodded. "And what a relief!"

"I told you that you didn't need that flower for courage, Carmen," Colby said, high-fiving me. "You were awesome!" He repeated that again, turning it into the chorus of one of his made-up songs.

"Thanks, Colby!"

Mr. Byrd came rushing onto the stage. "Great job, everyone! I couldn't be more proud of your performance!"

"Benton Bluff Junior High band!" Mrs. Dillingham came over, too. "I want to commend you for your hard work!"

Then she turned to Mr. Byrd. "You've done an outstanding job with this band."

"Thank you," Mr. Byrd said. "But I can't take any of the credit for tonight's show. All of the accolades belong to someone else."

I knew where Mr. Byrd was going with this. I turned toward Natalie and grinned. She'd really stuck by our band in the last few weeks. And she helped us when we needed it most!

But I couldn't believe it when Mr. Byrd said, "Band, let's give Carmen a hand to let her know we all appreciate her hard work on our musical score."

Everyone clapped. And Mr. Byrd must've noticed how surprised I was. "Natalie and I stayed in close contact while I was away," he said. "She told me how hard you worked on your own. And about some of the difficulties you faced. Please tell me how you pulled it off, Carmen."

"It was hard sometimes," I said. "I thought a lot about the differences in the holidays that people celebrate. But they have a lot in common, too. Like family and special services and stuff. Everyone in our band is different, too." I smiled. "But at the same time, we all love music. And our band director."

"Both of our band directors!" Hope added.

Natalie smiled, and said, "Thank you! I've enjoyed hanging out in room 217."

And Mr. Byrd said, "I'm pretty crazy about you guys, too."

"Hey, Mr. Byrd!" Davis said. "Do you know something else all of the different holidays have in common?"

Mr. Byrd shook his head. "What's that, Davis?"

"Yummy food! I'm starved," Davis said.

"Leave it to Davis!" I smiled.

"Let's go eat!" Sherman agreed.

Looking around, everyone was smiling. Instead of being a band divided, we were a band united. Again.